JUDY MOODY AND FRIENDS

Rocky Zang in
The Amazing Mr. Magic

Megan McDonald

illustrated by Erwin Madrid

based on the characters
created by Peter H. Reynolds

CANDLEWICK PRESS

For the original Rocky Zang

M. M.

For my brother, Edward,
and sister-in-law, Pitchie

E. M.

Text copyright © 2014 by Megan McDonald
Illustrations copyright © 2014 by Peter H. Reynolds
Judy Moody font copyright © 2003 by Peter H. Reynolds

Judy Moody®. Judy Moody is a registered trademark of Candlewick Press, Inc.

First edition 2014

Library of Congress Catalog Card Number 2012947727
ISBN 978-0-7636-5716-1 (hardcover)
ISBN 978-0-7636-7028-3 (paperback)

13 14 15 16 17 18 CCP 10 9 8 7 6 5 4 3 2 1

Printed in Shenzhen, Guangdong, China

This book was typeset in ITC Stone Informal.
The illustrations were created digitally.

Candlewick Press
99 Dover Street
Somerville, Massachusetts 02144

visit us at www.candlewick.com

CONTENTS

CHAPTER 1

The Amazing Mind Reader 1

CHAPTER 2

The Best Backyard Magic Show Ever 19

CHAPTER 3

The Disappearing Dollar 43

CHAPTER 1
The Amazing Mind Reader

Abracadabra! Kalamazoo!

Rocky had a magic wand. Rocky had a black top hat. Rocky had a long, dark cape. Meet the Amazing Mr. Magic!

Rocky could make a hankie change colors. Rocky could make a flower appear out of thin air. Rocky could make his very own thumb fly across the room.

The Amazing Mr. Magic was *almost* ready for the Best Backyard Magic Show Ever. The last thing he needed was one really good card trick. The Vanishing Ace? The Floating Joker? *Aha!* The Amazing Mind Reader!

Just then, his across-the-street best friend, Judy Moody, rode her bike down the sidewalk. *Alla kazam!* He could practice the trick on her.

"Hey, Judy. Pick a card," said Rocky. "Any card. But don't tell me what it is!"

"Okay," said Judy. "Now what?"

"Now put the card back."

Judy put the card back.

"Now I'm going to mix the cards all up. Then I'll read your mind and pull your card from the deck. Prepare to be amazed."

Rocky shuffled the cards.
Rocky closed his eyes. Rocky said,
"Hocus pocus, Jiminy bebop."

"Are those *real* magic words?" Judy asked.

"Shh. The Amazing Mr. Magic needs quiet to read your mind." Rocky pulled a card from the middle of the deck.

"Was it the ace of spades?"

"Nope. The queen of hearts," said Judy.

"Rats," said Rocky. "Try again?"

"Okay." Judy picked another card and put it back.

Rocky shuffled the deck.

Rocky closed his eyes.

He said the magic words.

Rocky pulled out a card.

"The jack of diamonds?" asked
Rocky.

"Nope. The two of clubs."

"Double rats," said Rocky.

He tried one more time. "The nine of hearts?" asked Rocky.

"Close. The six of spades," said Judy.

"I guess I stink at card tricks."

"I know a card trick that works every time," said Judy.

"Does it have magic words?"

"Sure."

"And you'll amaze me?"

"Double sure."

"*And* you'll read my mind?"

"This trick has it *all*," said Judy.

"What's it called?"

"Let's call it . . . Red Riding Hood and the Wolf. You be Red Riding Hood and I'll be the wolf."

"Why can't *I* be the wolf?" asked Rocky.

"Fine. You be the wolf," said Judy. "I'll be Red Riding Hood. So, first Red Riding Hood goes like this. . . ."

Judy tossed all fifty-two cards up into the air. Fifty-two cards came raining down helter-skelter.

"Next, the wolf picks them up,"
said Judy.

"Are you cuckoo? I'm not picking
up all those cards."

"Please?" Judy asked.

"No way."

"Okay, but if you don't pick them up,
how will you do any more card tricks?"
One by one by one, Rocky picked
up all fifty-two cards. Judy cracked up.

"That's not a card trick," said Rocky.
"That's a card *prank*. A real card trick
has magic words."

"I said *please*," said Judy. "*Please* is a magic word."

"A real card trick should astound and amaze you," said Rocky.

"It *amazed me* that you picked up all fifty-two cards," said Judy.

"You didn't even read my mind," said Rocky.

"Your mind was saying you did not want to pick up all those cards. Am I right?"

Rocky stared at Judy.

"See? It worked. I got you to pick up all fifty-two cards. That's the trick."

"Hmmm. . . . You know, every good magician needs an assistant," Rocky said, smiling.

Judy grinned.

Rocky could not wait to play the new card trick on somebody. Anybody.

Judy's little brother, Stink, was karate-kicking in the Moodys' front yard.

"Hey, Stink," Judy said. "Want Rocky to show you a card trick?"

"Sure," said Stink.

"It's called Billy Goat Gruff and the
Troll," said Rocky. "I'll be Billy Goat
Gruff. *You* be the troll."

CHAPTER 2
The Best Backyard Magic Show Ever

Rocky had on his black top hat.

Rocky had on his long, dark cape.

Rocky got out his magic wand.

Magic show time!

Rocky looked around. The backyard
was empty except for Judy Moody.

"Where is everybody?" Rocky
asked Judy.

"Frank had swim practice," said
Judy. "And Amy and Jessica Finch are
washing pets at the humane society."

"Who ever heard of a magic show without people to watch it?" Rocky asked. "Run and get Stink."

Judy ran across the street. Rocky waited.

In no time, Judy plopped Stink onto the picnic bench in Rocky's backyard.

"I'm the only one here?" Stink asked.
"Weird."

"The Best Backyard Magic Show Ever will now begin," Rocky said in a loud voice.

"I'm not picking up cards again," said Stink. "JSYK. Just So You Know."

"No card tricks. I promise," said
Rocky. "I'm the Amazing Mr. Magic,
and this is my assistant."

"Stella the Spectacular," said Judy.

"My first trick is called the Thrill-a-
fying Top Hat." Rocky pointed to the
empty table covered with an old sheet.

Rocky took off his hat. Rocky set his
hat on the table. He waved his magic
wand over the hat.

"I will close my eyes and Judy—I mean, Stella the Spectacular—will pour water into my hat. Then, when she puts the hat back on me— ta-da!—I will not get wet."

Rocky closed his eyes. He waited for Stella the Spectacular to pour the glass of water—not *in* his hat but *behind* his hat. *Way super tricky!*

He heard Stella the Spectacular begin to pour the water.

"Hey!" yelled Stink. "She's not pouring the water in the hat."

"Am so," said Judy.

"Are not," said Stink.

"Am too," said Judy.

Rocky did not hear water being poured. He opened his eyes. He stared straight ahead at Stink.

"And now, without further ado," he said, "Stella the Spectacular will place the hat on my head. And I, the Amazing Mr. Magic, will not get wet. Not one single drop of water."

Stink cracked up. Judy shrugged. In one swoop, she put the hat on Rocky's head.

Ker-splash!

Water rushed and gushed out of
the hat. Water drenched Rocky's hair.
Water dripped down Rocky's face.
Stink fell on the ground laughing.

Rocky glared at his assistant. "Why didn't you pour the water where I told you to pour the water?" Rocky asked between clenched teeth.

"Eagle-Eyed Stink was watching me like a hawk! I had to pour it into the hat."

Rocky wiped his face on his cape.

"The show must go on," said Rocky. "For my next trick, the Amazing Mr. Magic will change this jar of peanut butter into a jar of jelly. I call it the Supersonic Switcheroo."

Rocky put the peanut-butter jar on the table. He placed a shoe box over the jar. He placed a red silk cloth over the shoe box.

Judy lifted the old sheet and hid
under the table.

"Abracadabra." Rocky tapped the red silk cloth with his magic wand. "Alla-ka-peanut-butter. Jelli-ka-zam!"

Rocky heard rustle-bustle noises under the table.

"Judy's under the table!" yelled Stink.

Rocky heard crinkle-wrinkle noises.
He smiled weakly at Stink.

At last, Judy gave him the secret
signal of three knocks from under the
table. Mr. Magic yanked off the cloth
and lifted up the shoe box.

Voilà!

Rocky gaped at the not-jelly jar.

Stink laughed and pointed. "That's not jelly. It's ketchup!"

Rocky poked his head under the table. "You were supposed to swap the jar of peanut butter with the jar of *jelly*."

"I know!" said Judy. "And YOU were supposed to bring a jar of jelly, NOT a bottle of ketchup, Mr. Magic."

Rocky smacked his hand to his forehead and groaned.

"This is the worst magic show ever!" said Stink. "The Supersonic *Flub*-a-roo!"

"Quiet in the peanut gallery," said Judy.

"I'm going home," said Stink. "Unless you can pull a rabbit out of that hat or something."

"Or something," said Judy.

"You can't leave yet," said Rocky. "Those were just *practice* tricks. I will now perform the Houdini-est of all magic tricks. Mr. Magic will, before your very eyes, pull a rabbit out of this empty hat."

Stink sat back down. "For real?"

"For real," said Rocky. "See? The hat is empty." Rocky held the hat out in front of him.

Judy ducked back under the table.
Rocky heard something go *squish.*

Mr. Magic said the magic words.
"Izzy-wizzy fuzzy-wuzzy. Abiyoyo.
Alla kazam kazoo." *Kazoo* was the
secret word. *Kazoo* was the cue for Judy
to push the rabbit through the trick
bottom of the hat.

Rocky peered into the hat.

No rabbit.

"Kazoo!" he said, louder this time.

"Bless you," said Stink.

"Ka-ZOO, not ka-CHOO," said Rocky.

At last, *pop!* Rocky saw a bunny
ear poke through the bottom of the hat,
and—Zing Zang Zoom-a-roo!—he
reached into the hat and pulled out a
stuffed rabbit . . .

covered in ketchup!

"VAMPIRE RABBIT!"

Screaming, Stink leaped up and ran
out of the yard. He screamed as he ran
across the street. He screamed all the
way inside the Moody house.

Judy came out from under the table.

Rocky's ears turned red. Rocky's face turned red.

"Sorry. I guess I sat on the ketchup," said Judy.

"Stella," said Rocky, "you are the most UN-spectacular assistant ever! You messed up all my magic tricks!"

"Not *all* of your tricks," said Judy. "One of your tricks was super-spectacular."

"It was?" Rocky asked.

"The Disappearing Pest trick," said Judy. "You made Stink disappear!"

CHAPTER 3
The Disappearing Dollar

SHAZAM! Rocky had a new magic trick.

He called Judy Moody. "Meet me at the manhole. Pronto."

Rocky ran out of his house. Judy ran out of her house. They met in the middle.

"Guess what!" Rocky told Judy. "I have a new magic trick. The best magic trick ever."

"Better than the disappearing Stink trick?" Judy asked.

"Way better," said Rocky. He stared at Judy. "Why do you have leaves in your hair?" he asked.

"I was raking leaves," said Judy. "I made one whole dollar." Judy waved a brand-spanking-new dollar bill in Rocky's face. "Want to go to the candy store?"

"I was just going to ask you if you had a dollar," said Rocky. "My new trick is called the Disappearing Dollar."

"But I get my dollar back, right?" asked Judy.

"Right," said Rocky.

Judy held out her dollar. *One whole dollar bill.* Rocky tried to take the dollar, but Judy did not let go.

"You'll get it back," said Rocky.
"Cross my heart. Magician's honor!"

At last, Judy handed over her
dollar.

"Behold!" said Rocky. "The
Amazing Mr. Magic is about to make
George Washington disappear—
poof—into thin air."

"I can't stand to watch!" said Judy.
She covered her eyes with her hands.

"You have to watch," said Rocky.

Judy uncovered her eyes. Rocky held up the dollar bill, snapping it nice and tight. "Ready? Now you see it. . . ."

Rocky crunched the dollar bill up in his hands like a gum wrapper. Judy winced.

"Now you don't!" Rocky opened his hands. His hands were empty. The dollar bill was G-O-N-E, gone! *Vamoose!*

Vanished into thin air!

"Wait. What? WOW!" said Judy. "How did you do that?"

"Magic," said Rocky.

"You're like the best magician ever! But my dollar. Where is it?"

Rocky shook his head. "I can't tell you. Then it wouldn't be magic!"

"But . . . I'm Stella the Spectacular," said Judy. "Your assistant. Remember?"

"I remember that Stella messed up all of my magic tricks. This is one trick she is NOT going to mess up."

"But I'm your best friend," said Judy.

Rocky shook his head. "My lips are zipped."

"C'mon, Zipper Lips. I got three blisters for that dollar." Judy held up her hand and showed off her three Band-Aids.

"Still no," said Rocky.

"I didn't wreck your magic tricks on purpose," said Judy.

"Still no," said Rocky.

"I'm leaving," said Judy.

Rocky crossed his arms. "So leave."

"Not without my dollar."

"I already gave it back," said Rocky.

"Did not," said Judy.

"Did too," said Rocky. "Magically."

"Ugh! You know what, Rock? I take it back. You're like the *worst* magician ever. And the worst *friend* ever. You're the Amazing Mr. Meanie! *And* a big fat dollar stealer!"

Rocky watched as Judy stormed off down the sidewalk. Boy, was she in a mood. She jammed her hands into her pockets. Then, Judy stopped dead in her tracks.

Rocky waited.

At last, he saw her pull something
from her pocket. Something crinkly.
Something crumply.

Finally, Judy spun around and ran back toward Rocky, waving her dollar bill in the air.

"You *are* the best magician ever, Rock," she said. "You made my dollar disappear. But then you made it reappear in my pocket! And I didn't even know! Why didn't you just tell me?" she asked.

"I didn't want to spoil the magic," said Rocky.